SBN 361 01557 7
Material in this book is derived from the WINNIE THE POOH books
written by A. A. Milne with illustrations by E. H. Shepard.
Published by Purnell, London, W.1.
Printed in Italy by Officine Grafiche A. Mondadori Editore
Verona

A WALT DISNEY CLASSIC

Winnie the Pooh and the Blustery Day

A Story by A. A. Milne

Adapted and designed by
Peter Sims
from the Walt Disney film

PURNELL

London, W.1.

ONE blustery day Winnie the Pooh decided to visit his thoughtful spot and on the way he made up a little hum, and it hummed something like this: Hum dum dum di di dum, hum, dum, dum. Oh the wind is lashing lustily, and the trees are thrashing thrustily, and the leaves are rustling gustily, so it's rather safe to say, that it seems . . . that it may turn out to be . . . it feels that it will undoubtedly . . . it looks like a rather blustery day today. It seems that it may turn out to be, feels that it will . . . undoubtedly . . . looks like a rather blustery day today.

Fortunately, Pooh's thoughtful spot was in a sheltered place and now he sat down and tried hard to think of something. While Pooh Bear was thinking a Gopher popped up out of his hole.

"If I was you, I'd think about skedaddlin' out of here," said the Gopher to Pooh.

"Why?" asked Pooh.

"Because it's Windsday," said the Gopher and popped back into his hole.

Pooh thought for a moment and then said to himself. "Windsday? Oh, ah . . . oh. Then I think I shall wish everyone a Happy Windsday, and I shall begin with my very dear friend, Piglet."

Now, Piglet lived in the middle of the forest, in a very grand house, in the middle of a beech tree, and Piglet loved it . . . .

Outside Piglet's house was a sign which once had said TRESPASSERS WILL BE PROSECUTED but now, because it had broken in half, only said TRESSPASSERS WILL. According to Piglet the house had belonged to his Grandfather, and Piglet said his Grandfather's name was Tresspassers Will. This was short, said Piglet, for Tresspassers William and his grandma had called him T.W. which was even shorter. Well, on this blustery day, the wind was giving Piglet a bit of a bother. Piglet said to himself, "I don't mind the leaves that are leaving, it's the leaves that are coming."

Just as he finished speaking he was swept up and blown along on a large leaf. As Piglet was being blown along he flew past Pooh Bear who was on his way to wish Piglet a Happy Windsday.

"Where are you going Piglet?" asked Pooh.

"That's what I'm asking myself. Where? Whew . . . shoops," said Piglet.

Pooh grabbed hold of Piglet's scarf as he flew by.

"Oh Pooh," cried Piglet.

"And what do you think you will answer yourself?" asked Pooh, rather worried.

"Oh Pooh, I'm unravelling," said Piglet.

And he was. His scarf unravelled and he went high into the air, as high as a kite, while Pooh was left on the ground holding the other end of the unravelling scarf.

The scarf went on unravelling until there was no scarf left, only a string of wool. Piglet quickly grabbed hold of the end of the string.

"Oh . . . that . . . that was a c . . . c . . . close one," said Piglet, softly.

"Hang on tight, Piglet," called Pooh who was running along the ground holding onto the other end of the string.

Piglet flew over fields and hedges and all the time Pooh was running along beneath him. They came, after a while, to Kanga's house and Roo, who was in his mother's pouch called.

"Look, Mama, look, a kite!"

"Oh my goodness," said Kanga," it's Piglet!"

"Happy Windsday, Kanga. Happy Windsday, Roo," said Pooh as he rushed by.

"Can I fly Piglet next, Pooh?" asked Roo.

But Pooh didn't hear him, he was going too fast.

Eeyore had spent most of the morning building a lean-to of sticks.

"That should stand against anything," he said as he put the last stick on the pile. But it didn't, because at that very moment along swept Pooh Bear and he went right through Eeyore's lean-to and left just a pile of sticks.

"Happy Windsday, Eeyore," said Pooh.

"Thanks for noticing me," said Eeyore.

On and on swept Pooh and Piglet. Pooh was being bounced along the ground.

Rabbit was picking carrots from his carrot patch when along came Pooh digging his feet into the ground.

"Happy Windsday, Rabbit," called Pooh.

"Pooh Bear stop. Oh, go back. Oh, no!" cried Rabbit. He picked up his wheel-barrow and ran after Pooh.

Pooh's feet dug up all Rabbit's carrots and they flew up into the air and landed in Rabbit's wheelbarrow. Rabbit was very pleased and said to himself,

"Next time, I hope he blows right through my rhubarb patch."

Suddenly Pooh was lifted right off the ground and flew along with Piglet. The two of them were blown right up to the window of Owl's house.

"Who, who, who, who is it?" said Owl, who heard Piglet knocking on the window.

"It's me. P-p-p-please, May I come in?" called Piglet.

"Well, I say now, someone has pasted Piglet on my window," said Owl.

Then Pooh bumped into the window.

". . . Pooh, too. This is a surprise," laughed Owl.

"Well it's very nice to see you both," said Owl.

The house was being blown backwards and forwards and Owl started to tell Pooh and Piglet about an even worse wind he remembered. Just then, the tree with Owl's house in fell down with a crash. Owl was asking Pooh if he had knocked the tree down, when along came Christopher Robin and Eeyore.

"What a pity, Owl, I don't think we will ever be able to fix it," said Christopher Robin.

"If you ask me, when a house looks like that, it's time to find another one," said Eeyore.

"Might take a day or two, but I'll find a new one."

Later the blustery day had turned into a very blustery night. Pooh Bear was in his house and heard a very strange noise outside. The noise sounded like this "Rrrrrrrr!"

"Oh . . . is that you Piglet?" said Pooh, rather frightened.

"Rrrrr," said the noise.

"Well tell me about it tomorrow, Eeyore," said Pooh as he jumped under the covers on his bed.

"Rrrrrr," said the noise again.

"Oh, come in, Christopher Robin," said Pooh.

Now Pooh, being a bear of very little brain, decided to invite the new sound in.

"Hello out there. Oh, I hope nobody answers," he said.

"Rrrrrr. Hello, I'm Tigger," said Tigger.

"Oh," said Pooh. "Oh . . . Oh . . . you scared me."

Tigger had bounced right on top of Pooh and knocked him onto the floor.

"Oh, sure I did. Everyone's scared of Tiggers. And who are you?"
laughed Tigger.

"I'm Pooh," said Pooh.

"Oh, ah, Pooh. Sure. Ah . . .! he said. "What's a Pooh?"

"You're sitting on one."

Tigger shook his head.

"I am? Oh, well, glad to meet ya. Name's Tigger," and he climbed off Pooh. "T–I . . . double guh—er. That spells Tigger."

"But what is a Tigger?" asked Pooh.

"Well, ha, ha, he asked for it. Ho, ho," said Tigger and sang this song.

". . . The wonderful thing about Tiggers is Tiggers are wonderful things. Their tops are made out of rubber, their bottoms are made out of springs, they're bouncy, trouncy, flouncy, pouncy, fun, fun, fun, fun, fun, but the most wonderful thing about Tiggers is I'm the only one. I'm the only one. Rrrrrrr."

"Then what's that over there?" asked Pooh pointing to the mirror.

"Huh? oh, hey, hey, look, look what a strange lookin' creature. Hmm. Look at those beady little eyes, and that pur-posti-rus chin, and those ricky-diculus striped pyjamas," said Tigger.

"Looks like another Tigger to me," said Pooh.

"Oh, no, it's not. I'm the only Tigger. Watch me scare the stripes offa this imposter."

Tigger growled into the mirror and saw himself growling back. He was so frightened that he hid under the table.

"Is he gone?" asked Tigger.

"Yes," said Pooh. "You can come out now, Tigger."

"I'm hungry," said Tigger.

Pooh asked if he liked honey, hoping he would say no.

"Tiggers love honey," said Tigger.

"Oh dear," said Pooh but gave Tigger a jar of honey.

Tigger dropped his paw into the honey and tasted it.

"Ugh, Tiggers don't like honey," he said.

"But you said that you liked . . ." said Pooh, but before he could finish Tigger said,

"Yeah, that icky, sticky stuff is only fit for Heffalumps and Woozles."

"You mean Elephants . . . and Weasels," said Pooh.

"That's what I said. Heffalumps and Woozles."

"Well, well, what do heff ah . . . ah . . . hallalaff, ah . . . what do they do?" asked Pooh.

"Oh, nothin' much. Just steal honey."

"Steal honey?" cried Pooh grabbing his honey pot.

"Yeah, they sure do. Well, I'd better be bouncing along now . . ." said Tigger, and off he went singing his song.

Pooh said goodbye to Tigger and thought about Heffalumps and Woozles. He got his gun and decided to guard his honey. As he marched up and down, Pooh talked to himself in the mirror.

"Oh hello. Am I glad to see you. It's more friendly with two. Now, you go that way and I'll go this way."

"You didn't see anything, did you? Neither did I."

Pooh marched for hour after hour after hour. Guarding his honey. The blustery day had now turned into a very rainy night. Pooh kept marching, until at last he fell fast asleep and began to dream. He dreamt about Heffalumps and Woozles and this is the song they sang:

"Heffalumps and woozles. Heffalumps and woozles . . . steal honey. Beware. Beware. They're black, they're brown, they're up, they're

down. They're in, they're out, they're all about. They're far, they're near, they're gone, they're here. They're quick and slick, they're insin-cere. Beware. Beware. Beware. Beware. Beware. A heffalump or

woozle is very confusil. A heffalump or woozle's very sly, sly, sly, sly, they come in ones and twosles, but if they so choozles, before your eyes

you'll see them multiply, ply, ply, ply. They're extraordinary, so better be wary, because they come in every shape and size, size, size, size. If

honey's what you covet, you'll find that they love it, because they'll guzzle up the thing you prize. They're green, they're blue, they're pink,

they're white. They're round, they're square, they're a terrible sight, they tie themselves in horrible knots, they come in stripes or polka dots. Beware, beware, be a very wary bear."

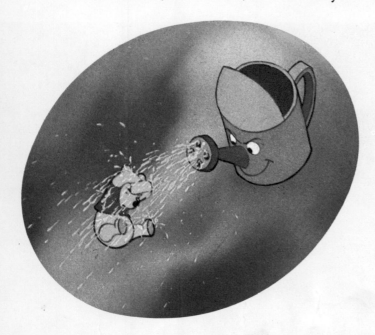

Outside Pooh's house it rained and rained and rained all through the night. When Pooh woke up in the morning his house was flooded with water, so he gathered up his honey pots and climbed the highest tree he could find.

Meanwhile Piglet's house had flooded too and Piglet had just written a note and put it in a bottle. The note said 'Help, Piglet' and Piglet had just put it in the bottle when he was washed right out of his house on a chair and along past Pooh sitting in the tree. Just then Pooh was knocked off his tree and landed in a honey pot. So Pooh in his honey pot and Piglet in his chair were swept along in the flood.

And the hundred acre wood got floodier and floodier. But the water couldn't come up to Christopher Robin's house . . . so that's where everyone was gathering. It was a time of great excitement. But in the middle of all the excitement Eeyore stuck stubbornly to his task of house-hunting for Owl.

Meanwhile, on Christopher Robin's island, Little Roo made an important discovery. He had found Piglet's note. Christopher Robin read the note and told everyone that Piglet was lost and they would have to rescue him. Owl flew off to search for Piglet and after a while he spotted Pooh and Piglet being swept along in the flood. He flew down and guided Pooh and Piglet back to Christopher Robin's island.

When they got to the island Pooh was sitting on the chair and Piglet had been swept into the honey pot.

"Hallo Pooh," said Christopher Robin. "Thank goodness you're safe. Have you seen Piglet?"

At that moment Piglet popped out of the honey pot.

"Excuse me, I have . . . Oh, what I mean is . . . here I am," said Piglet.

"Pooh you rescued Piglet," said Christopher Robin.

"I did?" said Pooh.

"Yes," said Christopher Robin, "you are very brave, and as soon as this flood is over I shall give you a hero party.

The next day the flood was over and everybody except Eeyore was at Christopher Robin's hero party for Pooh. Christopher Robin was saying:

"Attention everybody, this is a hero party for Pooh."

When along came Eeyore.

"I found it," he said.

"Found what, Eeyore?" asked Christopher Robin.

"A house for Owl," said Eeyore, "follow me."

They all followed Eeyore and he took them to Piglet's house.

"Why are you stopping here, Eeyore?" asked Christopher Robin.

"This is it," said Eeyore.

"Oh, dear. Mercy me," said Piglet.

"Name's on it," said Eeyore. "W – O – L spells Owl."

"Bless my soul, so it does," said Owl.

"Well, what do you think of it?" asked Eeyore.

"It is a nice house Eeyore, but . . ." said Christopher Robin.

"It is a lovely house . . ." said Kanga, "Eeyore, but, but . . ."

"It's the best house in the whole world," Piglet sobbed.

"Tell them it's your house, Piglet," said Pooh.

"No, Pooh," said Piglet. "This house belongs to our very good friend, Owl."

"But Piglet, where will you live?" asked Rabbit.

"Well, I . . . I–I–I guess I shall live ah . . . (sniff) I–I–I– suppose I–I– shall live . . ." sniffed Piglet.

"With me. You shall live with me, won't you, Piglet?" cried Pooh.

"With you? Oh, thank you, Pooh Bear. Of course I will," said Piglet.

"Piglet, that was a very grand thing to do," said Christopher Robin.

"A heroic thing to do," said Rabbit.

"Christopher Robin, can you make a one-hero party into a two-hero party?" asked Pooh.

"Of course we can, silly old bear," said Christopher Robin.

So Pooh was a hero for saving Piglet, and Piglet was a hero for giving Owl his grand home in the beech tree, and the two heroes had a lovely party with all their friends.

And so the blustery day turned out to be not so bad after all.